What Eats What

Katie Peters

GRL Consultants,
Diane Craig and Monica Marx,
Certified Literacy Specialists

Pull Ahead Readers

Lerner Publications ◆ Minneapolis

Note from a GRL Consultant
This Pull Ahead leveled book has been carefully designed for beginning readers. A team of guided reading literacy experts has reviewed and leveled the book to ensure readers pull ahead and experience success.

Lerner Publications Company
A division of Lerner Publishing Group, Inc.
241 First Avenue North
Minneapolis, MN 55401 USA

For reading levels and more information, look up this title at www.lernerbooks.com.

Main body text set in Memphis Pro 24/39
Typeface provided by Linotype.

Photo Acknowledgments
The images in this book are used with the permission of: © iStockphoto, pp. 3, 10–11, 16 (top center); © Shutterstock, pp. 4–5, 6–7, 8–9, 12–13, 14–15, 16 (top left), 16 (top right), 16 (bottom left), 16 (bottom right)

Front cover: © Shutterstock

Library of Congress Cataloging-in-Publication Data

Names: Peters, Katie, author.
Title: What eats what / Katie Peters.
Description: Minneapolis : Lerner Publications, [2019] | Series: Science all around me (Pull Ahead Readers. Nonfiction) | Audience: Ages 4–7. | Audience: K to grade 3. | Includes index.
Identifiers: LCCN 2018057828 (print) | LCCN 2019008785 (ebook) | ISBN 9781541562233 (eb pdf) | ISBN 9781541558502 (lb : alk. paper) | ISBN 9781541573284 (pb : alk. paper)
Subjects: LCSH: Food chains (Ecology)—Juvenile literature.
Classification: LCC QH541.15.F66 (ebook) | LCC QH541.15.F66 P48 2019 (print) | DDC 577/.16—dc23

LC record available at https://lccn.loc.gov/2018057828

Manufactured in the United States of America
2-51162-46231-6/9/2021

Contents

What Eats What

This bug is hungry.
What will it eat?
It eats plants.

This frog is hungry.
What will the frog eat?
It will eat the bug.

The snake is looking for something to eat.

It sees the frog.

The snake will eat the frog.

The hawk is hungry.
It looks for something to eat.
It sees the snake.
The hawk will eat the snake.

The bug eats the plant.
The frog eats the bug.
The snake eats the frog.
The hawk eats the snake.

What do you eat?

Did You See It?

bug

frog

hawk

snake

Index